For my mum
*–D.B.*

For Andy, Caroline,
Charlotte, and Harry
*–T.W.*

**tiger tales**
an imprint of ME Media, LLC
202 Old Ridgefield Road, Wilton, CT 06897
Published in the United States 2006
Originally published in Great Britain 2005
By Little Tiger Press
An imprint of Magi Publications
Text copyright ©2005 David Bedford
Illustrations copyright ©2005 Tim Warnes
CIP data is available
ISBN-10: 1-58925-058-3
ISBN-13: 978-1-58925-058-1
Printed in Belgium
1 3 5 7 9 10 8 6 4 2

# I've Seen Santa!

by David Bedford

Illustrated by
Tim Warnes

tiger tales

It was Christmas Eve,
and Little Bear was looking
forward to seeing Santa.
"Is Santa as big as you?"
he asked Big Bear.

"Nearly," said Big Bear, proudly.

"Oh," said Little Bear, looking worried.
"Will Santa fit down our chimney, then?"

"Of course he will!" said Big Bear. "I'll show you."

Big Bear went outside and climbed into
the chimney . . .

# CRASH!

"See?" said Big Bear, from a cloud of soot.
"Santa will get in, no problem!"

"Santa won't come if he sees this mess!"
said Mommy Bear.
"We'll help clean up," said Little Bear.

"Does Santa visit bears
all over the world?"
said Little Bear.
"Yes," said Big Bear.
"He goes to every
house."

"Hmm," said Little Bear. "He might not have time to come here, and then I won't have any presents."
"Don't worry," said Mommy Bear. "Santa will come just as soon as you go to sleep."

For SANTA
(paws off,
Big Bear)

Little Bear didn't want to go to sleep.
He wanted to see Santa. He listened to
Mommy Bear and Big Bear going to bed.
And then . . . . GLUG, GLUG, GLUG, GLUG!

What was that noise?
Someone was downstairs!

Someone big was sitting
by the fireplace.
"Yes!" whispered Little Bear.
"It's Santa! I've seen Santa!"
Little Bear tiptoed up and saw . . .

# Big Bear!

"That's Santa's milk!" said Little Bear.
"I only wanted a sip," said Big Bear,
"before I go to sleep." He took Little
Bear's hand. "Come on, Little Bear.
Let's go to bed."

Little Bear tried to stay awake, but he soon began to doze.

Then a loud noise downstairs woke him up.

MUNCH!

MUNCH!

MUNCH!

MUNCH!

Someone big was
standing by the
Christmas tree.
This time it had to be . . .

Big Bear again!

"You're eating Santa's blueberry
pies now!" said Little Bear.
   "I was hungry," said Big Bear.

"If Santa's as greedy as you,"
said Mommy Bear, coming
downstairs, "he really WILL
be too big to fit down the
chimney! Now go to bed
and go to sleep—
both of you!"

Little Bear went to bed, but he couldn't go to sleep. He was too worried. He woke up Big Bear to ask him a question.

"What if Santa eats too many blueberry pies and then gets stuck in the chimney?" he whispered.

"Hmm," said Big Bear.

"Let's keep watch to make sure he's OK," said Little Bear. "We can hide so he won't see us."

"Shhh!" whispered Little Bear
from their hiding place.
"I can hear something.
It MUST be Santa this time!"

Someone was putting
presents in their stockings!
Big Bear turned on his
flashlight to see . . .

# Mommy Bear!

"What are YOU doing?" said Big Bear.
    "I'm giving you both a present from me,"
said Mommy Bear. "What are YOU doing?"
    "We're not going to bed," said Big Bear.
    "We're going to see Santa!"
squealed Little Bear.

        Mommy Bear laughed.
    "Make room for me,
then," she said. "We'll
    ALL see Santa."

Little Bear, Big Bear, and
Mommy Bear stayed downstairs
all through the night.

But they never did see Santa . . .

even though
Santa saw them!